PUFFIN BOOKS
Published by the Penguin Group: London, New York, Australia,
Canada, India, Ireland, New Zealand and South Africa
Penguin Books Ltd, Registered Offices: 80 Strand, London WC2R 0RL, England

puffinbooks.com

First published 2013
001
Characters and artwork are the original creation of Tove Jansson
Text and illustrations copyright © Moomin Characters™, 2013
All rights reserved
Made and printed in China
Hardback ISBN: 978-0-723-27226-7
Paperback ISBN: 978-0-723-27227-4

MOOMIN

and the
Little Ghost

BASED ON THE ORIGINAL STORIES BY

Tove Jansson

PUFFIN

The moon shone high over Lonely Island.
The Moomins were holidaying at the
lighthouse, but Moomintroll couldn't sleep.
His bed wasn't like the one back home in the
Moominhouse and it was dark all around.

Even worse, he could hear strange noises
and he was sure he could hear the sound
of little scuttling feet.

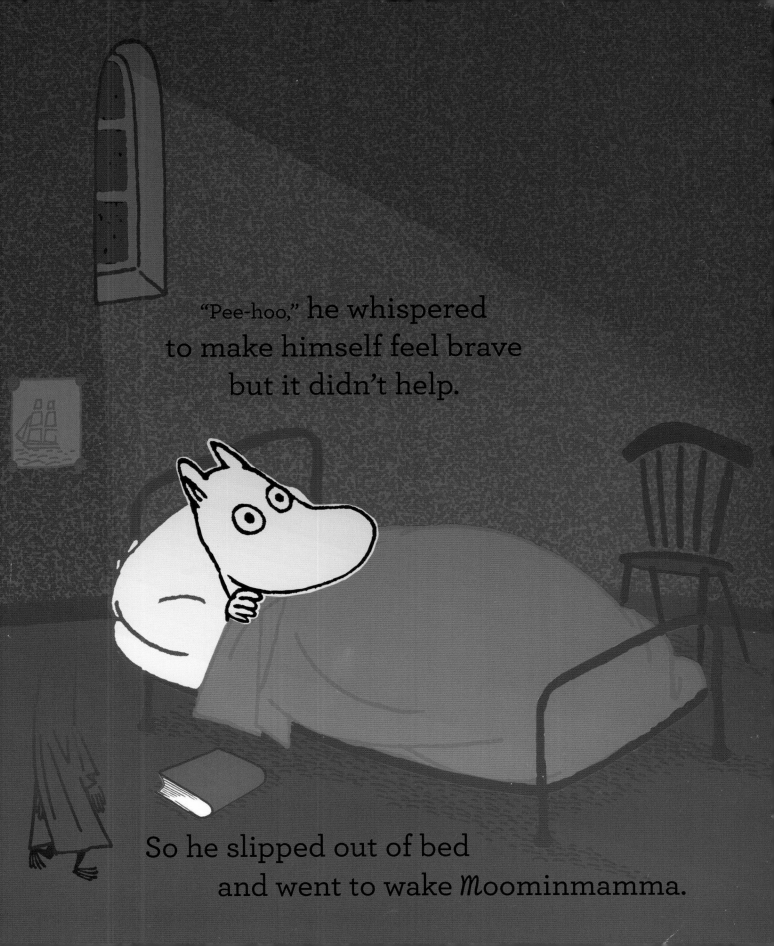

"Pee-hoo," he whispered
to make himself feel brave
but it didn't help.

So he slipped out of bed
and went to wake Moominmamma.

"Moominmamma," he said. "I can't sleep. It's ever so dark and I think I heard footsteps. I'm sure it must be a little ghost."

"Don't be scared, my little Moomin," said Moominmamma. "Let's put a little light by your bed. That will keep any old ghost away."

And together they went back to his bedroom.

"Did everyone sleep well?"
asked Moominpappa at breakfast.

"No," said Moomintroll. "I did NOT.
Not *even* with the light on. I think
there's a ghost in this lighthouse."

"Oh good!" said
Little My. "Is it very
frightening? I'll bite
it in the leg!"

"Don't be silly," said Snorkmaiden. "You can't bite ghosts."

"But I really did hear footsteps," said Moomintroll, "and I'm sure I even saw some little feet!"

"I think you should forget all about ghosts, Moomintroll," said Moominmamma.
"Why don't you go down to the beach and find Tooticky? You can take her some pancakes."

Down on the beach, Moomintroll suddenly turned to Snorkmaiden in fright.

"Look!" he said. "There are the spooky feet I told you about! There *is* a ghost, even in the daytime."

"That's no ghost," said Snorkmaiden. "That's Tooticky."

"Oh," said Moomintroll, embarrassed. "Tooticky, do you believe in ghosts?"

"Of course," said Tooticky. "But you needn't be frightened. The only dangerous thing about a ghost is being afraid of it."

And that made Moomintroll feel more worried than ever.

That night, Moomintroll was still scared,
despite the little lantern by his bed.
He heard creaking and rattling and he
was sure he saw the little feet again.

The same thing happened
the next night and
the next . . .

"Pee-hoo," he whispered
to make himself feel brave
but it still didn't help.

As the days passed, Moomintroll grew quieter and quieter and Snorkmaiden grew more and more worried.

So she went to find Tooticky . . .

"Tooticky," said Snorkmaiden, "how can I stop Moomintroll being so scared? He doesn't even want to have adventures any more."

"What we need," said Tooticky, "is a plan to show Moomintroll just how brave he is. And then he'll stop being afraid of ghosts."

And that gave Snorkmaiden an idea.

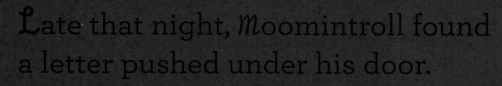
Late that night, Moomintroll found
a letter pushed under his door.

He opened the envelope
and found a note
from Snorkmaiden.

It said . . .

Dear Moomin,
   I have gone for a
moonlight walk by myself.
I didn't ask you to come
because I thought you
would be scared.
I shall be back by ten.
   Love,
      Snorkmaiden xx

"But that was two hours ago!"
thought Moomintroll with alarm.
"I must find her at once."

And he rushed out into the night,
his heart pounding with fear.

"I'm not scared of you, Ghost!"
he called to make himself
feel brave, following its
footprints in the sand.

At last Moomintroll came to the opening of a huge dark cave. Lying at his feet, he saw Snorkmaiden's anklet.

"She must be inside," he thought anxiously. "How scared she must be!"

Bravely, *Moomintroll* entered the
cave and called out,
"Don't worry, Snorkmaiden.
I have come to rescue you!"

But suddenly there was
the little ghost!

"Whoo! Whoo!"
it wailed, hoping to
scare *Moomintroll*.

But, instead of being scared, Moomintroll said,
"I'm sorry, I haven't got time to be frightened.
I'm very busy finding Snorkmaiden."
And, as he said it, two wonderful
things happened . . .

the little ghost vanished away . . .
and Snorkmaiden suddenly
appeared, safe and sound.

Moomintroll thought his heart
would burst!

When Moomintroll and Snorkmaiden got back to the lighthouse, everyone wanted to hear about their adventure.

"But weren't you scared?" asked Little My.

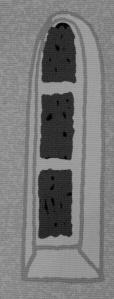

"Yes, I was," said Snorkmaiden. "But I knew *Moomintroll* would come and find me, even though he was scared of the ghost. Because, you know, he's really so *very* brave." And she hugged him close.

Moomin finished his cocoa and went upstairs with Moominmamma.

"I am very proud of you, my little Moomintroll," she said, tucking him into bed.

"We're going back home to the Moominhouse tomorrow, so you won't be scared of the ghost any more. Shall I leave the lantern by your bed?"

"No thank you, Mamma," said Moomintroll happily. "I'm not scared any more."

And he snuggled down under the blankets and slept soundly until morning.

The End